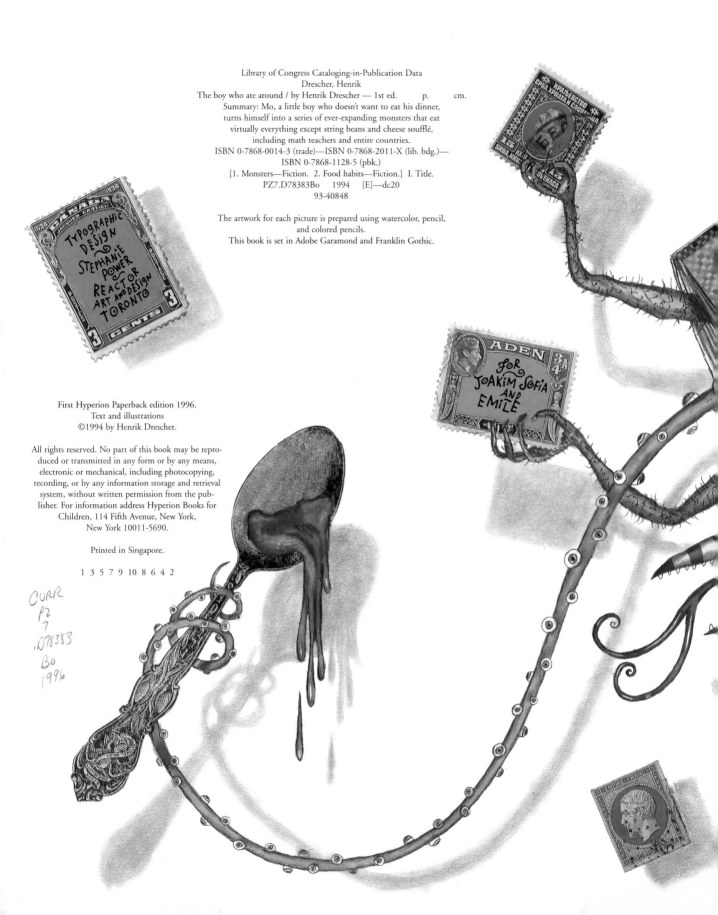

Library of Congress Cataloging-in-Publication Data
Drescher, Henrik
The boy who ate around / by Henrik Drescher — 1st ed.   p.   cm.
Summary: Mo, a little boy who doesn't want to eat his dinner,
turns himself into a series of ever-expanding monsters that eat
virtually everything except string beans and cheese soufflé,
including math teachers and entire countries.
ISBN 0-7868-0014-3 (trade)—ISBN 0-7868-2011-X (lib. bdg.)—
ISBN 0-7868-1128-5 (pbk.)
[1. Monsters—Fiction. 2. Food habits—Fiction.] I. Title.
PZ7.D78383Bo   1994   [E]—dc20
93-40848

The artwork for each picture is prepared using watercolor, pencil,
and colored pencils.
This book is set in Adobe Garamond and Franklin Gothic.

First Hyperion Paperback edition 1996.
Text and illustrations
©1994 by Henrik Drescher.

Printed in Singapore.

1 3 5 7 9 10 8 6 4 2

TYPOGRAPHIC
DESIGN
STEPHANIE
POWER
REACTOR
ART AND DESIGN
TORONTO

FOR
JOAKIM SOFIA
AND
EMILE

There once was a boy named Mo who had to eat his dinner even though he didn't like it **one** little **bit**.

He took a bite of the **lizard** guts and **bullfrog** heads

(ACTUALLY STRING BEANS AND CHEESE SOUFFLÉ)

and *felt* like **THROWING IT** all up, right there on the dinner TABLE, **but** he was polite and **DIDN'T.** **INSTEAD, he** decided to eat *around it.*

Then he **ate** the table and chairs.
(CRUNCHY!)

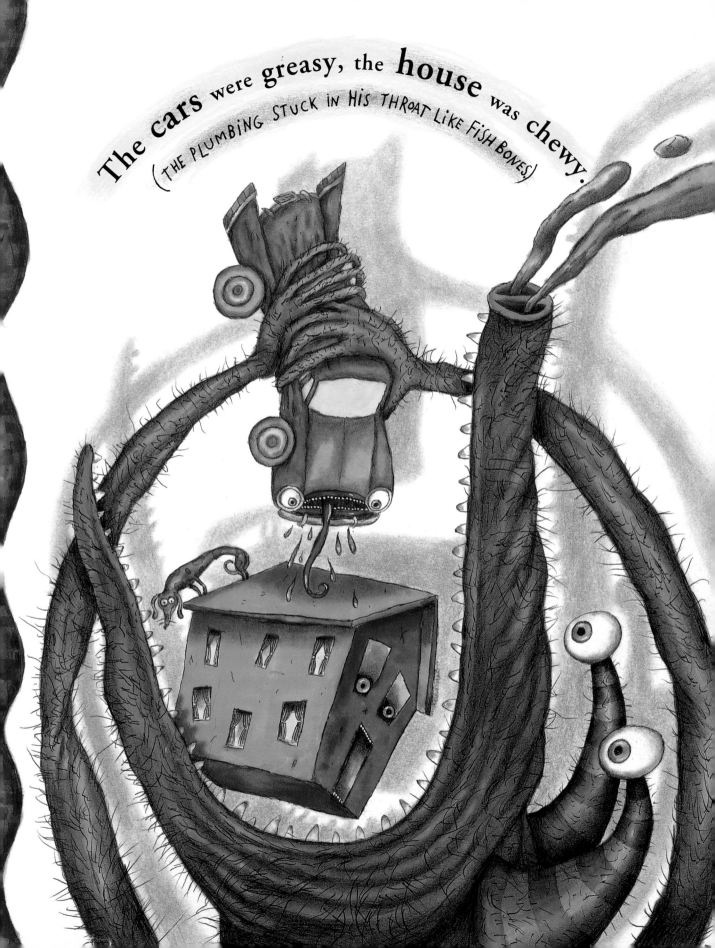

The cars were greasy, the **house** was chewy.
(THE PLUMBING STUCK IN HIS THROAT LIKE FISH BONES.)

Next he swallowed the neighbor's **cat,** followed by the **neighbor** and his **wife.**

When there was **no more** room left in the **belly** of the warthog monster,

he changed into something more comfortable —

a very **large** scaly *pink-eyed* **alligator chirper** –

and proceeded to **devour** his school, kids and all.

His **math** teacher he **saved** for last. (YUCK!!!)

To get the bad taste out of his mouth, he ate his best friend, Theo.

He then **munched** down the rest of the town

the **mall**, and **city hall**.

His **belly** was now **tight** as a **drum** with **all** that **was in it,** so he changed into a **humongous** bug-eyed **Slime Slusher** and ate the **White House,** the **President,** the **First Lady,**

First Dog, and **First Frog.** (WARTY!)

After which he devoured the whole country, state by state. Every town and

WASHINGTON

OREGON

IDAHO

MONTANA

N.DAKOTA

MINNESOTA

NEVADA

WYOMING

S.DAKOTA

NEBRASKA

VT. N.H. MASS. CONN. R.I.

COLORADO

KANSAS

MISSO

UTAH

ARIZONA

NEW MEXICO

OKLAHOMA

ARKA

TEXAS

The East he dipped into the Great Salt Lake. The North he peppered

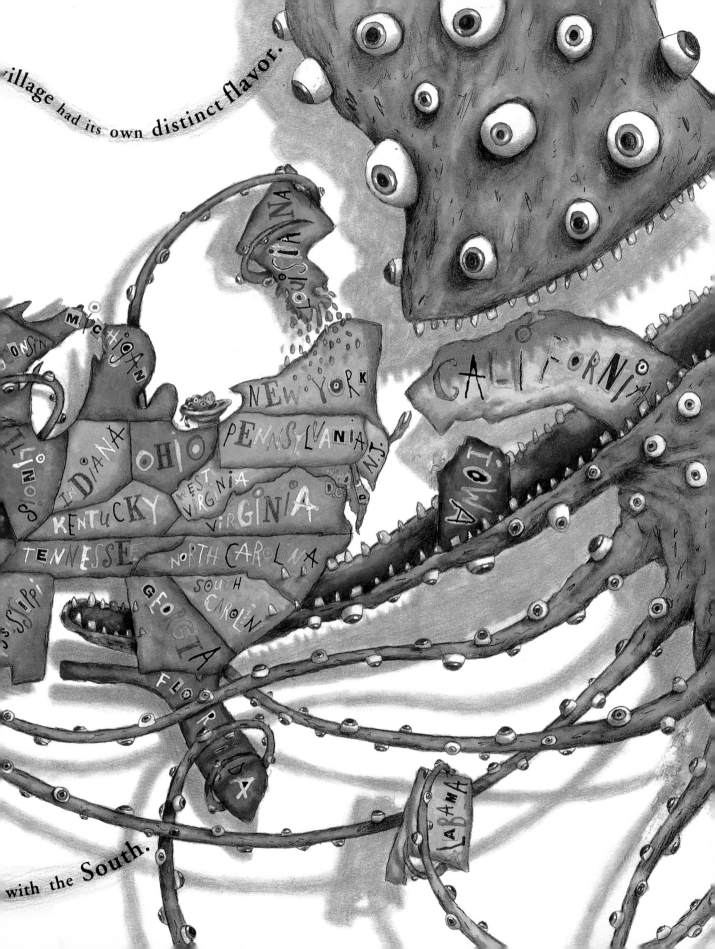

The **Rocky** Mountains he licked up like a **snow cone**

(WITH GRAVEL SPRINKLES

A nice **appetizer** he thought.

(BURP!

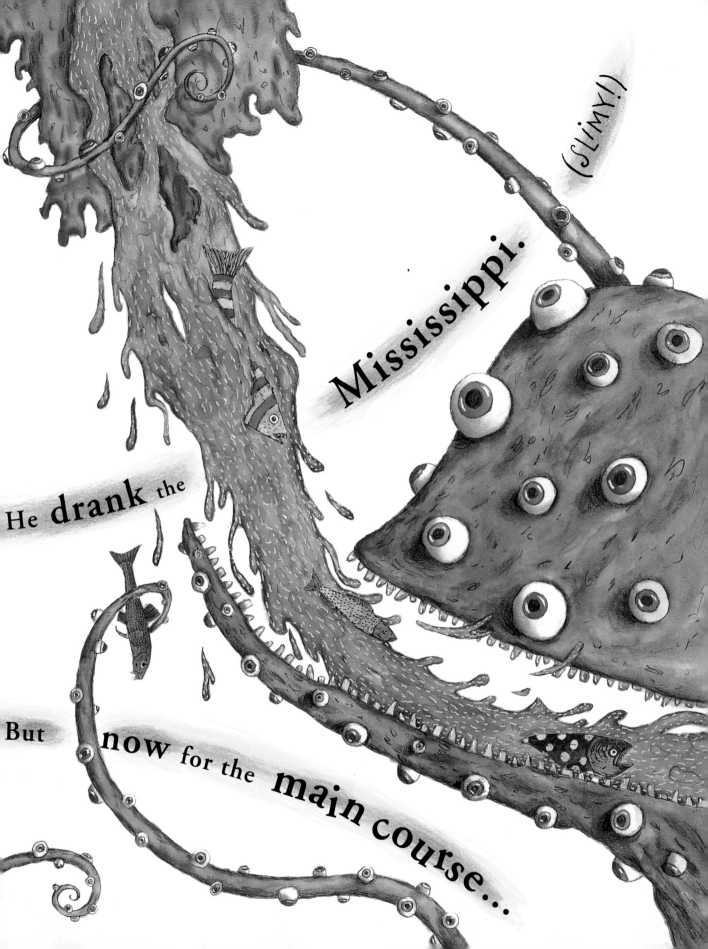

That was
a job
for a
truly
monstrous
belly!

He turned himself into a

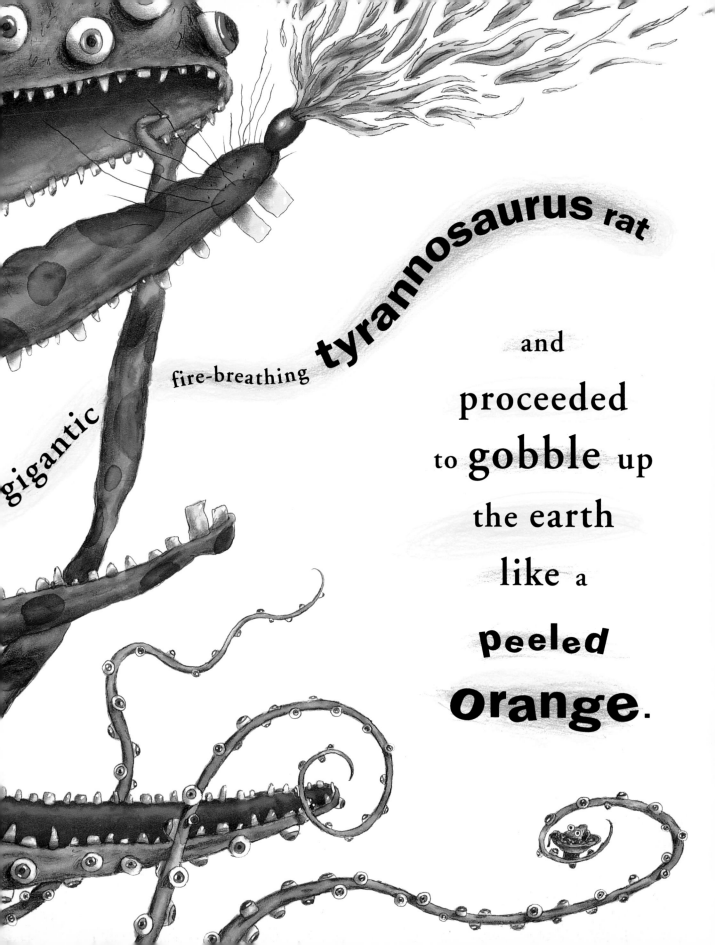

gigantic

fire-breathing **tyrannosaurus rat**

and
proceeded
to **gobble** up
the earth
like a
peeled
orange.

First he gulped down **China,** **wall** and all,

then **India.** *(Spicy!)*

He feasted on *smidgen of Holland, fricassee of France, slice of Italy.* *(GOOEY!)*

INDIA POSTAGE

Around the world he **chomped**, and the smaller it got, the **fatter** he grew.
Dessert was the **South Pole**.

For a midnight snack he rolled South America up ir

Africa, swallowing them whole like an enchilada.

When he was done, there was **nothing** left of the **world**, which left him hanging. **Just** him, the **moon**, and the plate of **string** beans and **cheese** soufflé. **With** a **swift** swat of his **tail**, he sent the dish **whirling**

...om the **moon.**

...at he had eaten around.

...to s p a c e .

He dangled there for a **moment** or two.
DIGESTING. STARGAZING. Passing the time
(AND SOME GAS!).
He felt **tired** and **lonesome.**

So he changed back into a **boy** named Mo and **poured** out all that was in the **huge** belly.

The countries,
the rivers,
his classmates,
the President,
the towns,
the people,
his teacher,
First Lady,
his neighbors, their cat,
First Frog and First Dog,
his best friend, Theo,

and *finally* his Mom and Dad, who were

It was decided that string beans and

Then they picked up Mo's best friend, Theo

very **happy** to see their little **rapscallion** again.

cheese **soufflé** were **off** the menu **forever.**

and went downtown for **banana splits**

(WHICH IS A NICE WAY TO END A BUSY DAY).

who ate

(Spicy!)

AND PROCEEDED TO DEVOUR HIS SCHOOL. KIDS AND ALL.

JAMAICA

EMILE

The boy

o's best friend, Theo, and went down

tring beans and cheese soufflé were

o see their little rapscallion again.

off the

own for

JOAKIM

(Slimy!)

Sweet!

(PICKY EATER!)

thanks to Howard REEVES

Space

Lonesome

Felt

TYRANNOSAURUS

around

dan
so
wa
Th
president, fi
teacher, his
his mom and

HIS MATH TEACHER HE SAVED FOR LAST (YUK!) TO GET THE BAD TASTE OUT OF HIS MOUTH. HE ATE HIS BEST FRIEND, THEO.

LANE

(Yuck!!!)

DATE DUE

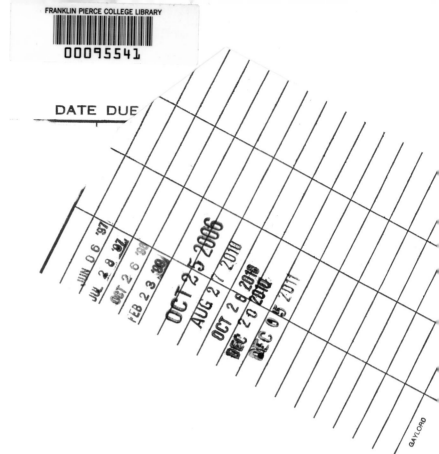